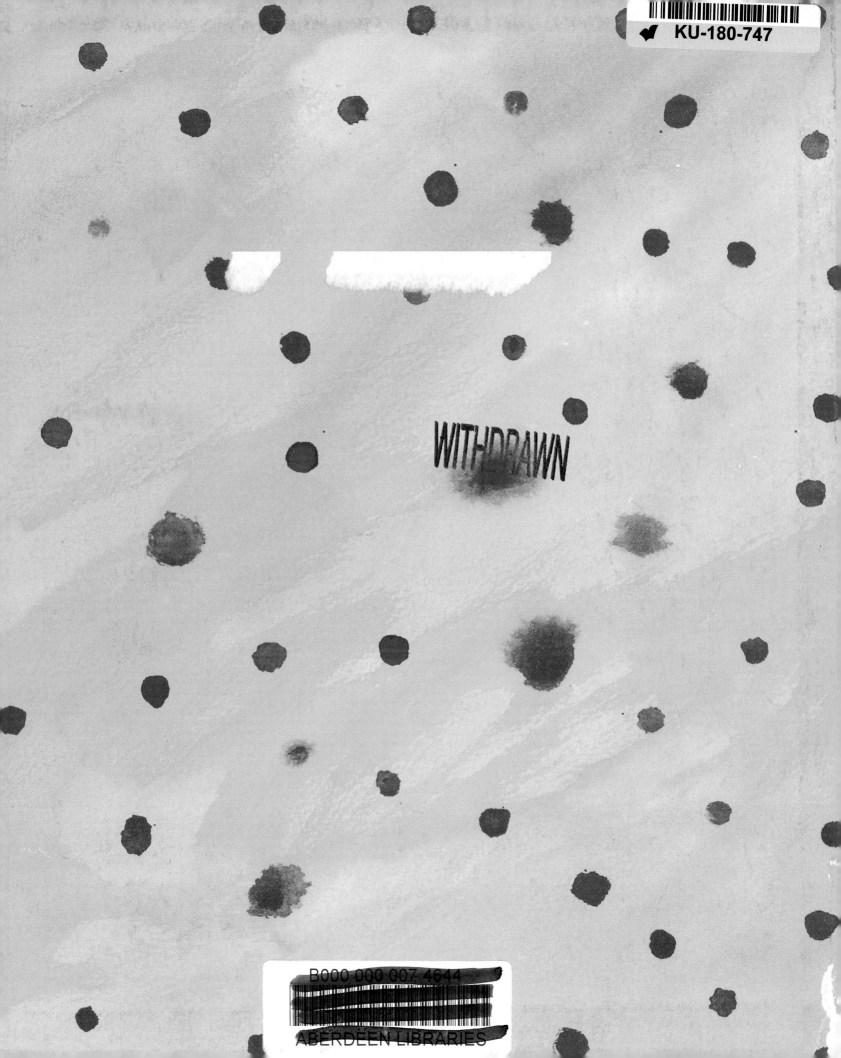

For Sian Wilkins: may all our
lumps and bumps be this benign.
J.W.

First published in Great Britain in 2012 by Andersen Press Ltd.,
20 Vauxhall Bridge Road, London SW1V 2SA.
Published in Australia by Random House Australia Pty.,
Level 3, 100 Pacific Highway, North Sydney, NSW 2060.
Text copyright © Jeanne Willis, 2012
Illustrations copyright © Tony Ross, 2012
The rights of Jeanne Willis and Tony Ross to be identified
as the author and illustrator of this work have been
asserted by them in accordance with the
Copyright, Designs and Patents Act, 1988.
All rights reserved.
Colour separated in Switzerland by Photolitho AG, Zürich.
Printed and bound in Singapore by Tien Wah Press.
Tony Ross has used pen, ink and watercolours in this book.

10 9 8 7 6 5 4 3 2 1

British Library Cataloguing in Publication Data available.

ISBN 978 1 84939 403 1 (hardback)

This book has been printed on acid-free paper

HIPPOSPOTAMUS

JEANNE WILLIS   TONY ROSS

ANDERSEN PRESS

Hippopotamus had a **spot**amus . . .

on her bottomus.

"It's Measles," said Weasel.
"You sat in a breezle
And caught a diseasel.
There's only one treatment,
Exposing your seatment
To sunshine and heatment."

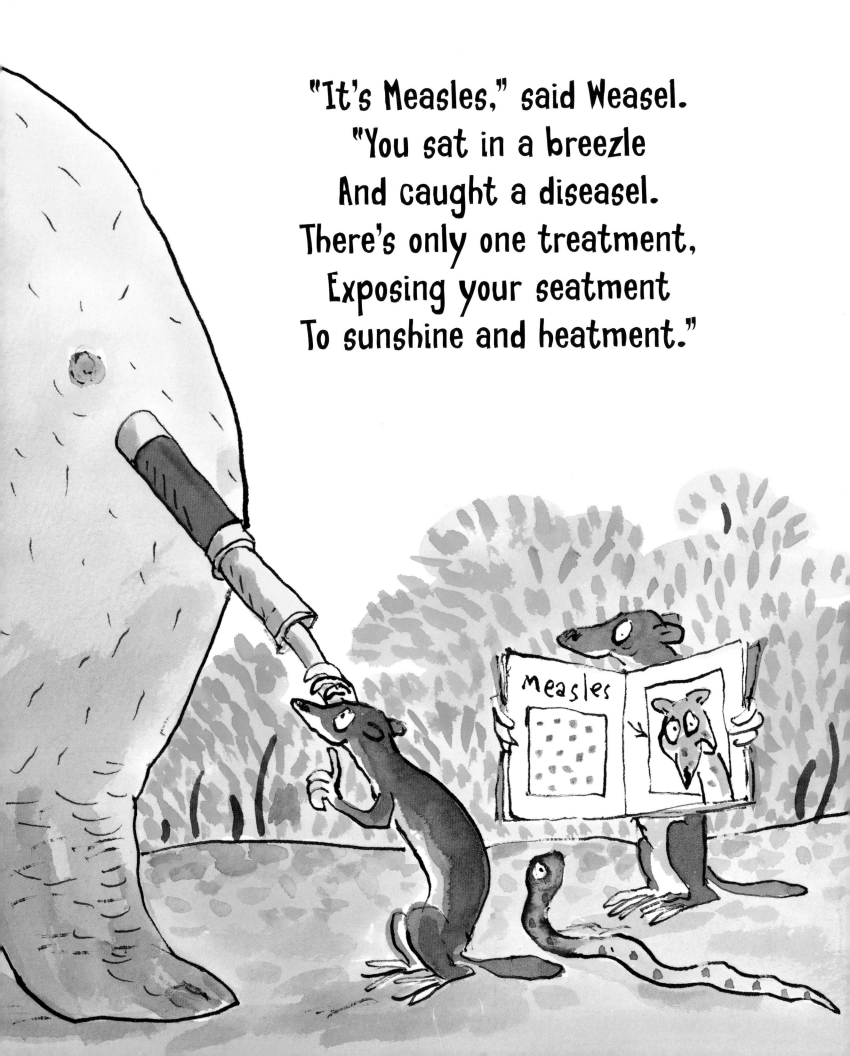

Potamus stood on her head
Tail to the sun like Weasel said.
But the **spot**amus stayed red.

"It's Hippopox!" said Fox.
"Wear woolly pants and socks.
Warm petticoats and frocks."

But Potamus got hotamus,
Grumpimus and grotamus
And still she had the **spot**amus.

"It's Jungle Fever!" said Beaver.
"I believe we should leave her
To scrub her skin with soot."

So Potamus got sootimus
From noseymus to footimus,
But the **spot**amus stayed put.

"It's Hippolumps!" said Lion.

"It's Potomumps!" said Shrew.

"It's Hippoflu!" said Rhino.

But no one had a clue.

"I'm a doctor," said the Croc.
"Do you feel any pain
When I stroke it?
And poke it?
Let me try that again.

A needle in the bottomus
Will rid you of the **spotamus**."

Despite his perfect shotamus,
The cure was in vain.

"It's a blister," said her sister.
"You should pop it right away."

"It's a trapped hair!" said Brown Bear.
"Just smother it with clay."

"It's notamus! What rottomus!
You clottomus!" hissed Snake.
"This lippy hippypotamus
Is allergic to cake.
Cut out chippochoccomus
Eat lettuce for a week."

But the spot on Hippo's bottomus
Stuck firmly to her cheek.

Then all sad and snottamus
There came a little lad
Who searched round alotamus
For something he once had.

He knew he'd put it somewhere
But, alas, he had forgottamus
Until he saw the botty
Of the spotty Hippopotamus.

The small boy had a sneaky peek
And tweaked the hippo's bum.
"That's not a spot!" he squeaked . . .

"That's my bubble gum!"